Our Celebración!

by **Susan Middleton Elya**

illustrations by

Ana Aranda

Lee & Low Books Inc. *New York*

Edited by Louise E. May
Designed by Christy Hale
Production by The Kids at Our House
The text is set in Pike and Opti Adrift
The illustrations are rendered in watercolor, gouache, and inks on watercolor paper
Manufactured in Malaysia by Tien Wah Press
10 9 8 7 6 5 4 3 2 1
First Edition
Library of Congress Cataloging-in-Publication Data
Names: Elya, Susan Middleton, author. | Aranda, Ana, illustrator.
Title: Our celebración! / by Susan Middleton Elya ; illustrations by Ana Aranda.
Description: First edition. | New York : Lee & Low Books Inc., [2018] |
Summary: A brief rain shower does not dampen a Latino family's enjoyment of their town's parade and summer
celebration, which includes street food, bands, a corn princess, and fireworks. Spanish words, interspersed in
the rhyming text, are defined in a glossary.
Identifiers: LCCN 2016042651 | ISBN 9781620142714 (hardback)
Subjects: | CYAC: Stories in rhyme. | Parades—Fiction. | Fairs—Fiction. | Summer—Fiction. | Hispanic Americans—Fiction.
Classification: LCC PZ8.3.E514 Ce 2018 | DDC [E]—dc23
LC record available at https://lccn.loc.gov/2016042651

To Peter and Naomi in Aspen—*S.M.E.*
To my parents, who taught me to celebrate life
and pursue happiness—*A.A.*

Today's a happy celebration,
a time for joy and jubilation.
Get your family—one, two, three.
Are you ready? **¡Claro! ¡Sí!**

No one's working, closed **tiendas**.
Bright balloons and **meriendas**.
All the buildings dressed so cool—
rojo, **blanco**, plus **azul**.
Count the dozens of **banderas**
as we climb **las escaleras**.

Un desfile down this street.
Wear your hat and grab a seat.
Yes, today's a party **día**.
Take a bite of pink **sandía**,
tacos, hot dogs, **hamburguesas**—
lots of laughter, fun **sorpresas**.

High above, from **el balcón**,
look what comes round **el rincón**—
rows of fast **motocicletas**,
lots of kids on **bicicletas**,
fire trucks with giant hoses
spraying folks, with sunburned noses.

Clarinetes, saxophone—
here comes music . . . **bón, bón, bón!**
Flautas, tubas, glockenspiel—
mothers smile and babies squeal.

Seventy-seven brass **trompetas**.
Now to make the band **completa**—
in the back, a row of drummers,
old-time jeeps and bright newcomers.

Queens in gold **coronas** smiling.
Girls on horses single filing.
Caballitos, dressed-up **perros**,
decorated **caballeros**.
Kids on scooters, tall **triciclos**,
boys on shiny **monociclos**.

See the grown-ups' big **sonrisas**.
Shadows fading, cooling **brisas**,
storm clouds forming overhead.
No! We want **el sol** instead.

Boys with carts sell lemonade.
Please don't rain on our parade!
Drops of **agua** from the clouds
fall on hot but happy crowds.

Clowns throw **dulces**. Mouths are drooling.
Feel the sizzling sidewalks cooling.
Duck for cover, form a huddle—
in **la calle**, splashy puddles.

ROJO ANARANJADO AMARILLO VERDE

Sun comes out, a lovely sight—
gives us seven stripes of light.
Make a wish and blow a kiss.
There's magic at a time like this.

The show is over. Take a stroll.
Let's eat **helado** from a bowl—
vanilla, chocolate, mint, or **fresa**.
Look! There goes the corn **princesa**.
Her brother's pig was Best in Show.
A purple ribbon—way to go!

Best pie bake-offs, rodeos,
three-legged races, talent shows,
chili cook-off, water fights,
fireworks for sparkling nights.
Pop, pop, pop—the dazzle zone.
Cannon fires—**explosión!**

¡**Sí**! Today's a special day.
Meet **vecinos**. Laugh and play.
For whatever good **razón**,
we love our **celebración**!

Glossary

(el) agua (AH-gwah): water

amarillo (ah-mah-REE-yoe): yellow

anaranjado (ah-nah-rahn-HAH-doe): orange

azul (ah-SOOL): blue

(el) balcón (bahl-KONE): balcony

(las) banderas (bahn-DEH-rahs): flags

(las) bicicletas (bee-see-KLEH-tahs): bikes, bicycles

blanco (BLAHN-koe): white

bón, bón, bón (bone, bone, bone): boom, boom, boom

(las) brisas (BREE-sahs): breezes

(los) caballeros (kah-bah-YEH-roce): cowboys

(los) caballitos (kah-bah-YEE-toce): ponies

(la) calle (KAH-yeh): street

(la) celebración (seh-leh-brah-SYONE): celebration

(los) clarinetes (klah-ree-NEH-tehs): clarinets

claro (KLAH-roe): of course

completa (kome-PLEH-tah): complete

(las) coronas (koe-ROE-nahs): crowns

(el) desfile (dehs-FEE-leh): parade

(el) día (DEE-ah): day

(los) dulces (DOOL-sehs): sweets

el, la, las, los (ehl, lah, lahs, loce): the

(las) escaleras (ehs-kah-LEH-rahs): stairs

(la) explosión (eks-ploe-SYONE): explosion

(las) fiestas (FYEHS-tahs): parties

(las) flautas (FLOU-tahs): flutes

(la) fresa (FREH-sah): strawberry

(las) hamburguesas (ahm-boohr-GHEH-sahs): hamburgers

(el) helado (eh-LAH-doe): ice cream

índigo (EEN-dee-goe): indigo (purplish blue)

(las) meriendas (meh-RYEHN-dahs): picnics

(los) monociclos (moe-noe-SEE-cloce): unicycles

(las) motocicletas (moe-toe-see-KLEH-tahs): motorcycles

(los) perros (PEH-rroce): dogs

(la) princesa (preen-SEH-sah): princess

(la) razón (rrah-SONE): reason

(el) rincón (rreen-KONE): corner

rojo (RROE-hoe): red

(la) sandía (sahn-DEE-ah): watermelon

sí (SEE): yes

(el) sol (SOLE): sun

(las) sonrisas (sone-REE-sahs): smiles

(las) sorpresas (sohr-PREH-sahs): surprises

(las) tiendas (TYEHN-dahs): stores

(los) triciclos (tree-SEE-cloce): tricycles

(las) trompetas (trome-PEH-tahs): trumpets

un, una (oon, OO-nah): a, an, one

(los) vecinos (veh-SEE-noce): neighbors

verde (VEHR-deh): green

violeta (vyoe-LEH-tah): violet